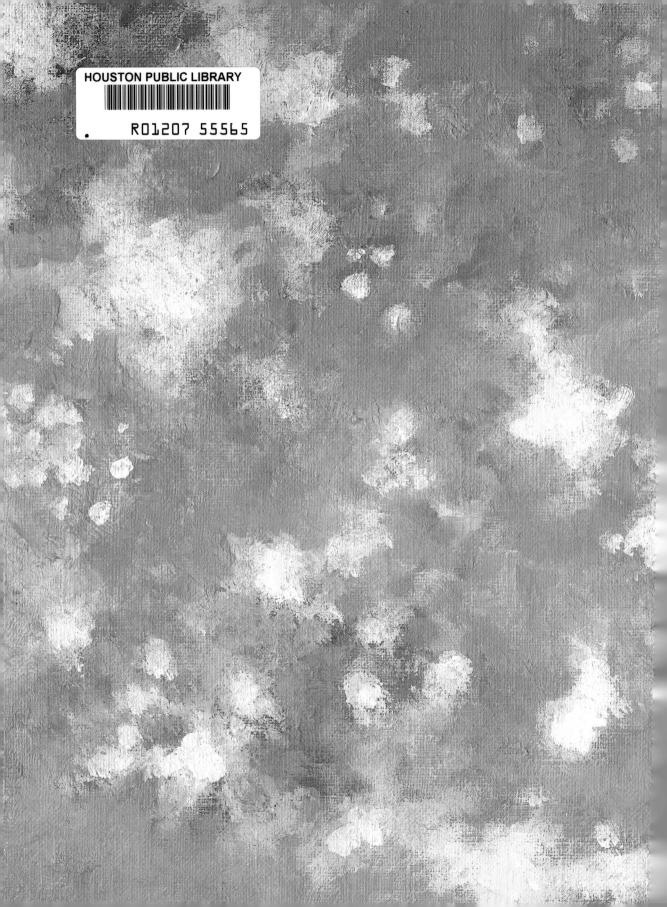

# 大鳥樹

文字・插畫／蘇珊・梅朵
Text & Illustrations by Susan Meddaugh
譯者／蔡佩宜

**晨星出版**

　　海瑞並沒有親眼看見鳥被車子撞到。他只聽到輕輕碰的一聲，等他回頭一看，她已經躺在地上了。她沒有死，只是翅膀看起來不大對勁，海瑞就把她撿起來帶回家。

Harry didn't see the car hit the bird. He heard a soft thunk, and when he turned around, there she was. She wasn't dead, but her wing didn't look quite right, so he picked her up and carried her home.

「媽咪。」海瑞說。

「喔，你回來了！」海瑞的媽媽說。

「她的名字叫做莎莉。」海瑞告訴媽媽。

"Oh, Mom," said Harry.

"Oh, my！" said Harry's mother.

"Her name is Sally," Harry told her.

3

　　海瑞小心的照顧莎莉。 他幫她包紮翅膀， 好讓她早點痊癒， 他還跑到寵物店買她的食物。

Harry took good care of Sally. He taped her wing so that it would heal. He went to the pet store and bought her food.

甚至，他跑去圖書館借了一些關於鳥的書。

　　「莎莉，妳知道妳是一隻熱帶綠冠鳥嗎？」他問莎莉。

　　「這時候妳應該已經飛去南方了，寒冷的天氣會凍死妳的！」

And he went to the library to take out some books about birds.

"Did you know you're a Green Tufted Tropical?" he asked Sally.

"You're supposed to be way down south this time of year. Cold weather could kill you!"

　　日子一天天的過去， 莎莉的翅膀很快就好了。 可是， 莎莉站在窗前，看著葉子從樹上掉下來， 看起來很難過的樣子。

Days passed, and Sally's wing was quickly healing. But Sally stood at the window, watching the leaves fall and looking sad.

海瑞的媽媽說：「莎莉吃得不多耶！」

「可能她吃膩了小蟲，」海瑞說，「也許她想改吃點蒼蠅。」

「也可能她很寂寞，」媽媽說。

Harry's mother said, "Sally isn't eating very much."
"Maybe she's tired of worms," said Harry. "Maybe she'd like some flies for a change."
"Maybe she's lonely," said his mother.

「　莎莉是一隻野鳥，」她說，「你也知道，你不能把她永遠留在身邊，她應該和她的朋友在一起。」

"Sally is a wild bird," she said. "You can't Keep her forever, you know. She belongs with her friends."

「　我就是她的朋友啊！」海瑞說。

"I'm her friend," said Harry.

　　第二天，　海瑞老是覺得怪怪的，好像有人在跟蹤他。　可是，　他每次轉身，　都沒有看到什麼人。

The next day, Harry had the strangest feeling that he was being followed. But every time he turned around, no one was there.

當天下午，他發現窗外的景象有些奇怪。雖然所有的樹都掉了葉子，卻有一棵樹愈變愈綠。那是熱帶特有的鮮綠色。

海瑞便到外面看個究竟。

That afternoon, he noticed something unusual outside his window. While all the other trees were losing their leaves, one tree was getting greener and greener. Bright tropical green.

Harry went outside to investigate.

等他走近時才發現，那棵樹並不是長滿了葉子，那是一整樹跟莎莉一樣的熱帶綠冠鳥。

When he got close to the tree he saw that it wasn't covered with leaves. It was a tree full of birds — Green Tufted Tropicals, just like Sally.

他ㄊ們ㄇ讓ㄖ海ㄏ瑞ㄖ覺ㄐ
得ㄉ很ㄏ不ㄅ舒ㄕ服ㄈ，所ㄙ以ㄧ
他ㄊ走ㄗ回ㄏ屋ㄨ裡ㄌ。

They made Harry uncomfortable, so
he went back into the house.

第<ruby>二<rt>ㄦ</rt></ruby><ruby>天<rt>ㄊㄧㄢ</rt></ruby>一<ruby>早<rt>ㄗㄠˇ</rt></ruby>，那<ruby>群<rt>ㄑㄩㄣˊ</rt></ruby><ruby>鳥<rt>ㄋㄧㄠˇ</rt></ruby><ruby>兒<rt>ㄦ</rt></ruby><ruby>們<rt>ㄇㄣˊ</rt></ruby><ruby>跟<rt>ㄍㄣ</rt></ruby><ruby>著<rt>˙ㄓㄜ</rt></ruby><ruby>海<rt>ㄏㄞˇ</rt></ruby><ruby>瑞<rt>ㄖㄨㄟˋ</rt></ruby><ruby>去<rt>ㄑㄩˋ</rt></ruby><ruby>上<rt>ㄕㄤˋ</rt></ruby><ruby>學<rt>ㄒㄩㄝˊ</rt></ruby>。

The next morning the birds followed Harry to school.

他們在外面等他，

They waited for him outside,

放學時，　他們又跟著海瑞回家。

and when school was over, they followed him home.

　　每天晚上，　鳥兒們都在海瑞窗戶外面的樹上棲息。

　　每天不管海瑞走到哪裡，　他們就跟到哪裡，　海瑞知道他們要的是什麼。「你們不能把莎莉要回去！」他告訴他們。

Every night the birds perched in the tree outside Harry's window.
Every day they followed him everywhere he went. Harry knew what they wanted. "You can't have Sally," he told them.

　　天氣愈來愈冷，　鳥兒們仍待在樹上不走，　似乎沒有任何事物可以說服他們往南飛。　風趕不走。

The days got colder. The birds stayed on. It seemed that nothing would convince them to fly south. Not wind.

雨ㄩˇ也ㄝˇ趕ㄍㄢˇ不ㄅㄨˋ走ㄗㄡˇ。

Not rain.

　　海瑞自己也沒辦法，　不過他仍然試一試。

　　起初，　他試著跟他們講道理。「莎莉是我的鳥兒，」他解釋說，「我把她照顧得很好，　所以，　現在你們可以走了。」　但是鳥兒們哪裡也不去。

Not Harry himself. But he tried.

First he tried to reason with them. "Sally is my bird," he explained. "I'm taking good care of her, so you can all go now." The birds didn't go anywhere.

海瑞還試著嚇跑鳥兒們。

Harry tried to frighten the birds away.

鳥‧兒‧們‧ 沒‧有‧上‧當‧。

The birds were not fooled.

海瑞懇求他們說：「你們不知道冬天快來了嗎？你們一定要趕快往南飛，不然會來不及，你們會活不過第一場暴風雪的！」

Harry pleaded with them: "Don't you know winter is coming? You've got to fly south before it's too late. You'll never survive the first snowstorm!"

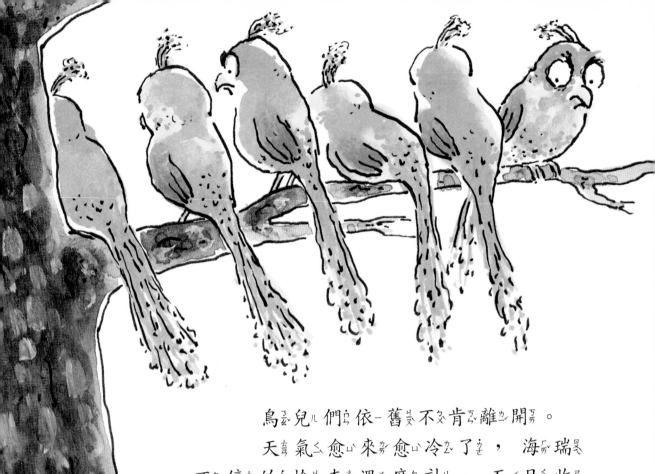

鳥兒們依舊不肯離開。

天氣愈來愈冷了，　海瑞不停的檢查溫度計，　而且收聽氣象報告。　然後有一天早上，　海瑞聽到了他最害怕聽到的話。　「快拿出你們的鏟子，」　氣象預報員說，　「一場大風雪快要來了！」

Still the birds wouldn't leave.

As the days grew colder, Harry found himself checking the thermometer and listening to the weather reports. Then one morning, Harry heard the words he had been dreading. "Get out your snow shovels," said the weatherman. "A big winter storm is coming our way!"

「笨鳥，大笨鳥！」他尖叫著。
「如果你們全凍死了，可不要怪我。」

"STUPID, STUPID BIRDS!" he screamed. "Don't blame me if you all freeze to death."

　　海ㄏㄞˇ瑞ㄖㄨㄟˋ懷ㄏㄨㄞˊ著ㄓㄜ˙沉ㄔㄣˊ重ㄓㄨㄥˋ的ㄉㄜ˙心ㄒㄧㄣ情ㄑㄧㄥˊ，　進ㄐㄧㄣˋ入ㄖㄨˋ他ㄊㄚ的ㄉㄜ˙房ㄈㄤˊ間ㄐㄧㄢ。

　　他ㄊㄚ看ㄎㄢˋ到ㄉㄠˋ莎ㄕㄚ莉ㄌㄧˋ注ㄓㄨˋ視ㄕˋ著ㄓㄜ˙窗ㄔㄨㄤ戶ㄏㄨˋ外ㄨㄞˋ的ㄉㄜ˙大ㄉㄚˋ鳥ㄋㄧㄠˇ樹ㄕㄨˋ。

　　「哦ㄛˊ，莎ㄕㄚ莉ㄌㄧˋ！」海ㄏㄞˇ瑞ㄖㄨㄟˋ說ㄕㄨㄛ，「妳ㄋㄧˇ這ㄓㄜˋ麼ㄇㄜ˙想ㄒㄧㄤˇ念ㄋㄧㄢˋ妳ㄋㄧˇ的ㄉㄜ˙朋ㄆㄥˊ友ㄧㄡˇ嗎ㄇㄚ˙？」

Harry went to his room with a heavy heart.

He saw Sally looking out at the tree of birds.

"Oh, Sally," Harry said. "Do you miss your friends so much?"

「哦ㄛˊ， 媽ㄇㄚ 媽ㄇㄚ 咪ㄇㄧ 呀ㄚ！」 海ㄏㄞˇ 瑞ㄖㄨㄟˋ 説ㄕㄨㄛ。

"Oh, Mom!" said Harry.

## 關於作者：

### 蘇珊・梅朵 Susan Meddaugh

生長於美國新紐澤西州，畢業於惠頓大學，主修法國文學和美術。曾在紐約的廣告公司工作過短期間，然後搬到波士頓，在出版社工作了十年。從一開始的設計師、美術編輯到最後成為美術總監之後，她決定辭職專心從事童書創作和繪畫，當一名童書的創作與插畫家。

她創作了許多受歡迎的童書，其中《 Martha Speaks 》獲選為1992年 New York Times 最佳繪本。她目前和丈夫、兒子住在麻州。

## 關於譯者：

### 蔡佩宜

淡江德文系畢業，從事業餘翻譯工作已有十五年歷史。初期曾為《世界地理雜誌》翻譯有四年之久。

譯作有《當火星男人愛上金星女人》(太雅生活館)、《男人來自火星，女人來自金星》(太雅生活館)等書。

小書迷 01

# 大鳥樹

| | |
|---|---|
| 文字・插畫 | 蘇珊・梅朵 Susan Meddaugh |
| 內封題字 | 葉 珊 小 朋 友 |
| 譯者 | 蔡 佩 宜 |
| 文字編輯 | 詹 雪 玉 ／ 馬 嘉 璐 |
| 美術編輯 | 劉 巧 玲 |
| 發行人 | 陳 銘 民 |
| 發行所 | 晨星出版社 |

台中市工業區30路1號

TEL:(04)3595820　　FAX:(04)3595493

E-mail:morning @ tcts.seed.net.tw

郵政劃撥：02319825

行政院新聞局局版台業字第2500號

| | |
|---|---|
| 法律顧問 | 甘 龍 強 律師 |
| 製作 | 知文企業（股）公司　TEL:(04)3595819-120 |
| 印刷 | 威文彩色印刷股份有限公司 |
| 初版 | 中華民國88年8月30日 |
| 總經銷 | 知己有限公司 |

〈台北公司〉台北市羅斯福路二段 79 號 4F 之 9

TEL:(02)23672044 FAX:(02)23635741

〈台中公司〉台中市工業區 30 路 1 號

TEL:(04)3595819　FAX:(04)3595493

定價200元

（缺頁或破損的書，請寄回更換）

ISBN 957-583-757-6

獻給——

框框之外的生命畫家